KATIE DAVIS

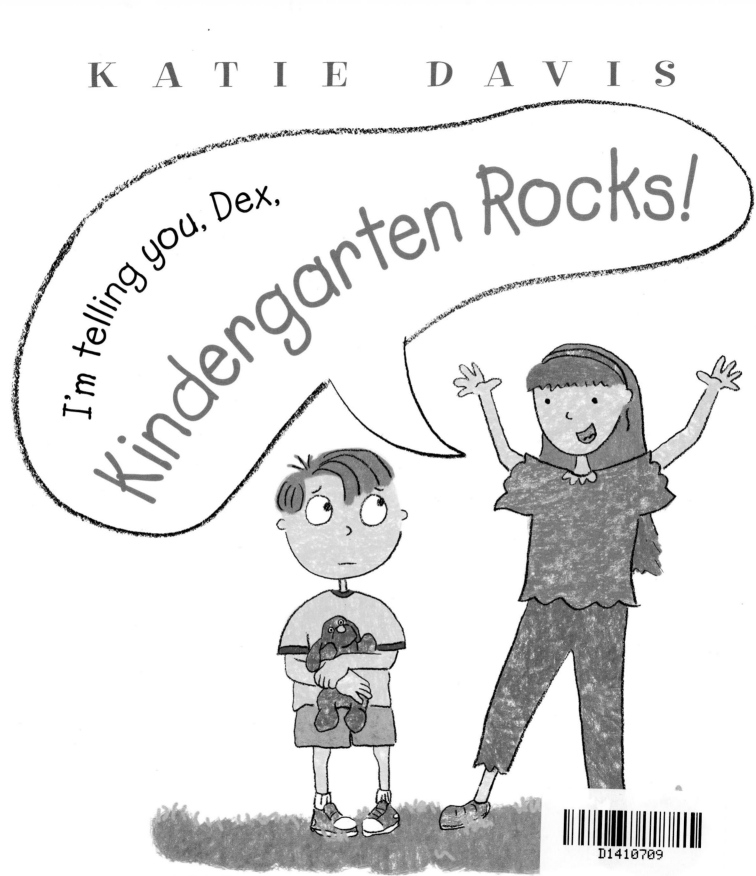

I'm telling you, Dex, Kindergarten Rocks!

VOYAGER BOOKS

HARCOURT, INC. • Orlando   Austin   New York   San Diego   London

D1410709

I am Dexter Dugan and I know everything about kindergarten. This is because I am actually going to *be* a kindergartner. Very soon.

To my former teachers Mrs. Cook, Mr. Saunders, and Mrs. Ciricillo;
to the fabulous teachers at my kids' school;
to all teachers who inspire and ignite our children every day
—K. D.

Special thanks to:
My children, Benny and Ruby, who let me use their artwork in the book.
Another to Ruby, who, based on her own kindergarten experience, came up with the title.
And Ms. Sugarman, for being an enthusiastic listener, guide, and model, and who is as sweet as her name.

Requests for permission to make copies of any part of the work should be submitted online at www.harcourt.com/contact
or mailed to the following address: Permissions Department, Harcourt, Inc., 6277 Sea Harbor Drive, Orlando, Florida 32887-6777.

www.HarcourtBooks.com

First Voyager Books edition 2008

Voyager Books is a trademark of Harcourt, Inc., registered in the United States of America and/or other jurisdictions.

The Library of Congress has cataloged the hardcover edition as follows:
Davis, Katie (Katie I.)
Kindergarten rocks!/written and illustrated by Katie Davis.
p.   cm.
Summary: Dexter knows everything there is to know about kindergarten and is not at all scared about his first day there, but his stuffed dog, Rufus, is very nervous.
[1. First day of school—Fiction.
2. Kindergarten—Fiction.
3. Schools—Fiction.]
I. Title.
PZ7.D2944Ki   2005
[E]—dc22   2003022623
ISBN 978-0-15-204932-4
ISBN 978-0-15-206468-6 pb

H G F E D C B

The display type was set in Lemonade Bold.
The text type was set in Elroy.
Color separations by Bright Arts Ltd., Hong Kong
Manufactured by Worzalla Publishing, U.S.A.
Production supervision by Christine Witnik
Designed by Linda Lockowitz

I'm going to learn lots of stuff in kindergarten,
but the thing I learned today was . . .

Rufus was so happy to see me. He knew I'd find him the whole time.

After lunch, everyone goes to recess. Joey says you can't get lost playing
I-Am-A-Monster-And-You-Are-A-Powerful-Monster-Getter
because if someone's always chasing you, how can you get lost?

And there are people called custodians who clean the whole entire school
and they help you even when you spill your milk by accident
and you are scared you'll get in trouble.

At lunch you get to eat with all your friends in the cafeteria.
It's exactly almost like a restaurant.

Then we went to the library. That's where you go if you want to know about snails or soccer or outer space or shark guts. You can borrow a whole book all about it and keep it practically forever.

I got to write letters,

and build a gigantic tower,

and play in the
imagination station,

and look at books.

We made art,

I think Rufus wants to lick the spoon.

and cooked food,

and smushed Play-Doh.

For one thing, my friend Joey from preschool was there.
Rufus was so happy to see him, he forgot to worry.

There are some *kind of* good surprises about kindergarten.

When we finally got to school, I couldn't wait to see my classroom.

Rufus was still worried, but Jessie had a great idea.

When the bus came the next morning,
the driver seemed like he knew what he was doing, so I got on.

I can't wait.

Kindergarten will be
a piece of cake.

Nooooo problem.

I got Jessie to help me make a list of things Rufus was scared about.

I'm not worried though.

She wrote like me. And she drew like me, too.

Only not as good.

When Jes went to kindergarten, she wasn't big like she is now.

Jessie went to kindergarten a long, long, long, long, long, long, long, long, long, long, long time ago (but she still remembers it even though she's going into third grade).

My dog Rufus is an eensy teensy beensy bit scared about kindergarten.